CAMP YOWIE

By Alexandria Gold, Ph.D.
Illustrated by Chris King

Publishing Credits

Rachelle Cracchiolo, M.S.Ed., *Publisher*
Conni Medina, M.A.Ed., *Editor in Chief*
Nika Fabienke, Ed.D., *Content Director*
Véronique Bos, *Creative Director*
Shaun N. Bernadou, *Art Director*
Noelle Cristea, M.A.Ed., *Senior Editor*
John Leach, *Assistant Editor*
Jess Johnson, *Graphic Designer*

Image Credits

Illustrated by Chris King

Library of Congress Cataloging-in-Publication Data

Names: Gold, Alexandria, author. | King, Chris (Illustrator), illustrator.
Title: Camp Yowie / by Alexandria Gold, Ph.D. ; illustrated by Chris King.
Description: Huntington Beach, CA : Teacher Created Materials, [2020] |
 Includes book club questions. | Audience: Age 9. | Audience: Grades 4-6.
Identifiers: LCCN 2019034792 (print) | LCCN 2019034793 (ebook) | ISBN
 9781644913673 (paperback) | ISBN 9781644914571 (ebook)
Subjects: LCSH: Readers (Elementary) | Camps--Juvenile fiction. |
 Sasquatch--Juvenile fiction.
Classification: LCC PE1119 .G5935 2020 (print) | LCC PE1119 (ebook) | DDC
 428.6/2--dc23
LC record available at https://lccn.loc.gov/2019034792
LC ebook record available at https://lccn.loc.gov/2019034793

Teacher Created Materials

5301 Oceanus Drive
Huntington Beach, CA 92649-1030
www.tcmpub.com

ISBN 978-1-6449-1367-3

Table of Contents

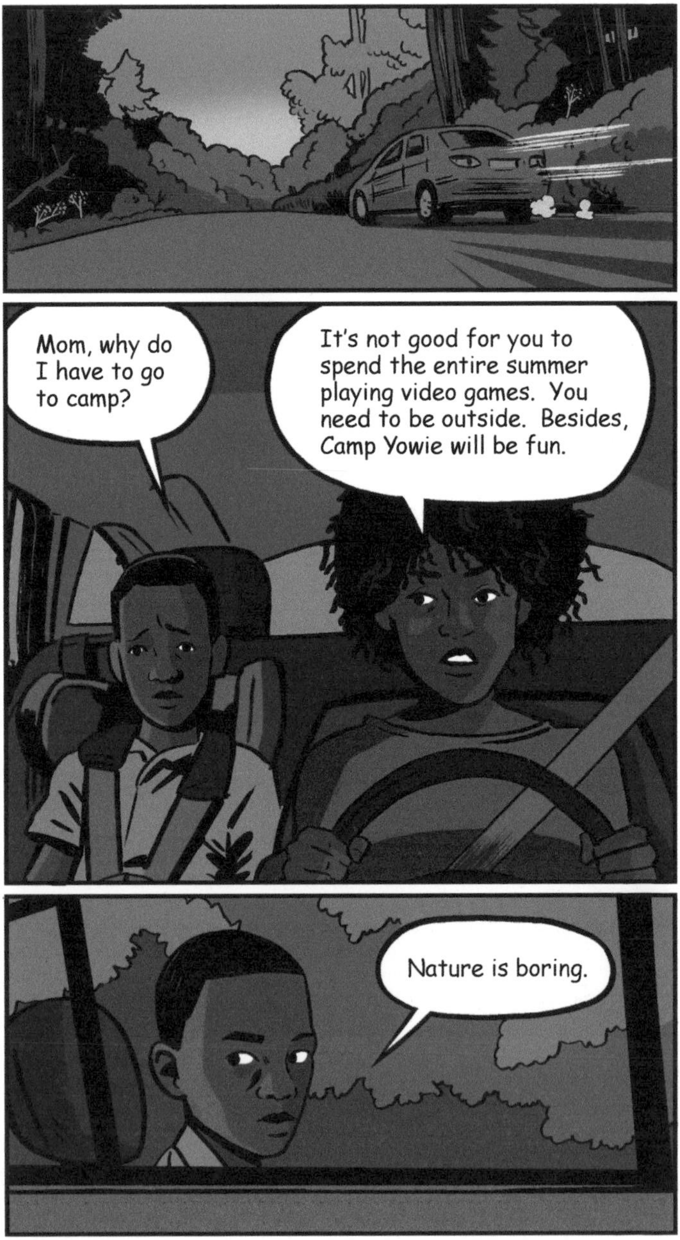
Mom, why do I have to go to camp?
It's not good for you to spend the entire summer playing video games. You need to be outside. Besides, Camp Yowie will be fun.
Nature is boring.

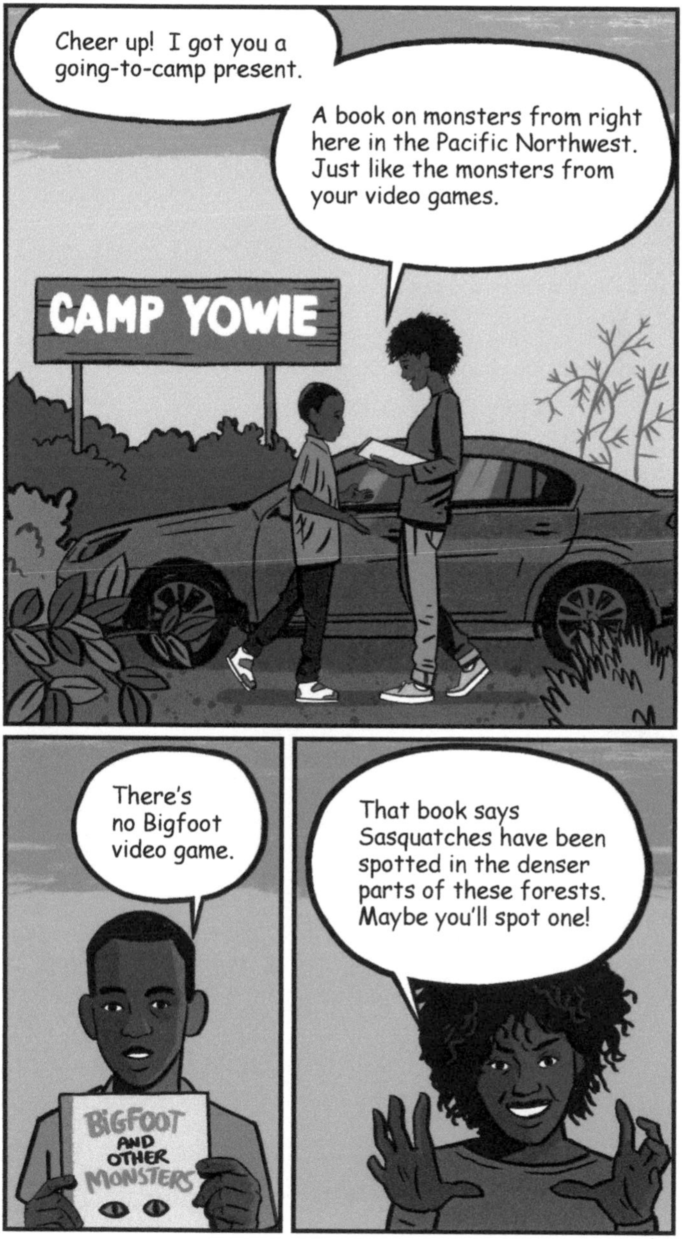
Cheer up! I got you a going-to-camp present.
A book on monsters from right here in the Pacific Northwest. Just like the monsters from your video games.
CAMP YOWIE
There's no Bigfoot video game.
BIGFOOT AND OTHER MONSTERS
That book says Sasquatches have been spotted in the denser parts of these forests. Maybe you'll spot one!

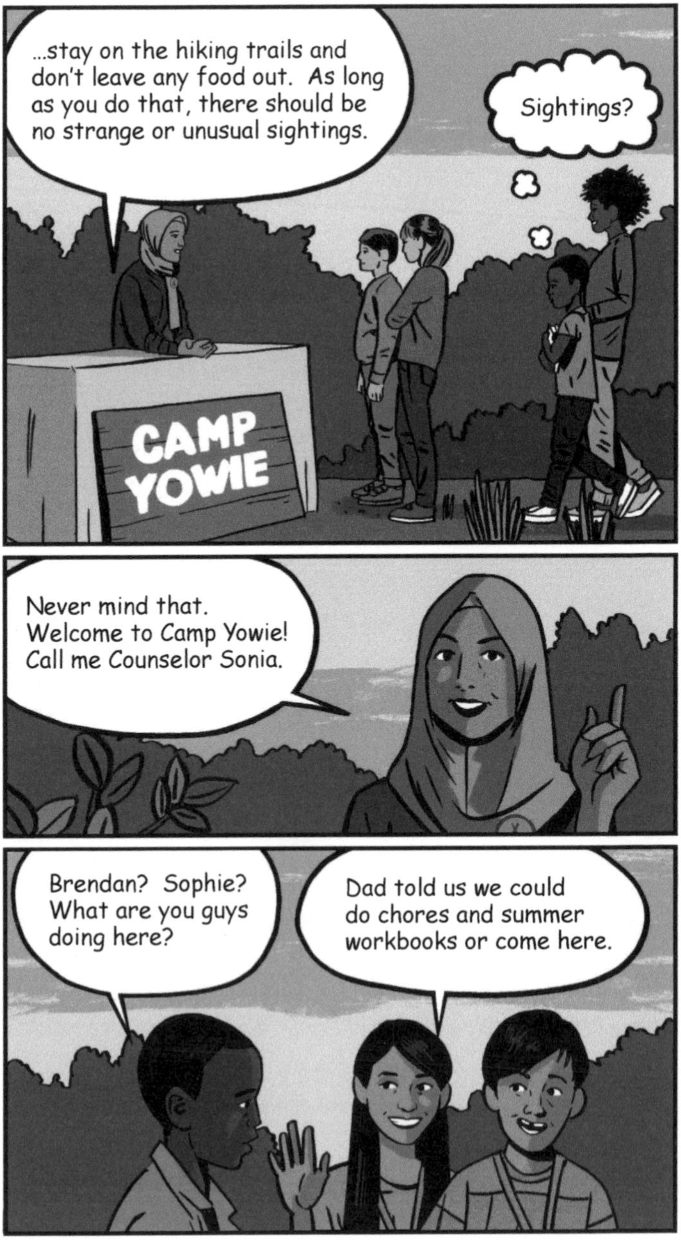
...stay on the hiking trails and don't leave any food out. As long as you do that, there should be no strange or unusual sightings.
Sightings?
CAMP YOWIE
Never mind that. Welcome to Camp Yowie! Call me Counselor Sonia.
Brendan? Sophie? What are you guys doing here?
Dad told us we could do chores and summer workbooks or come here.

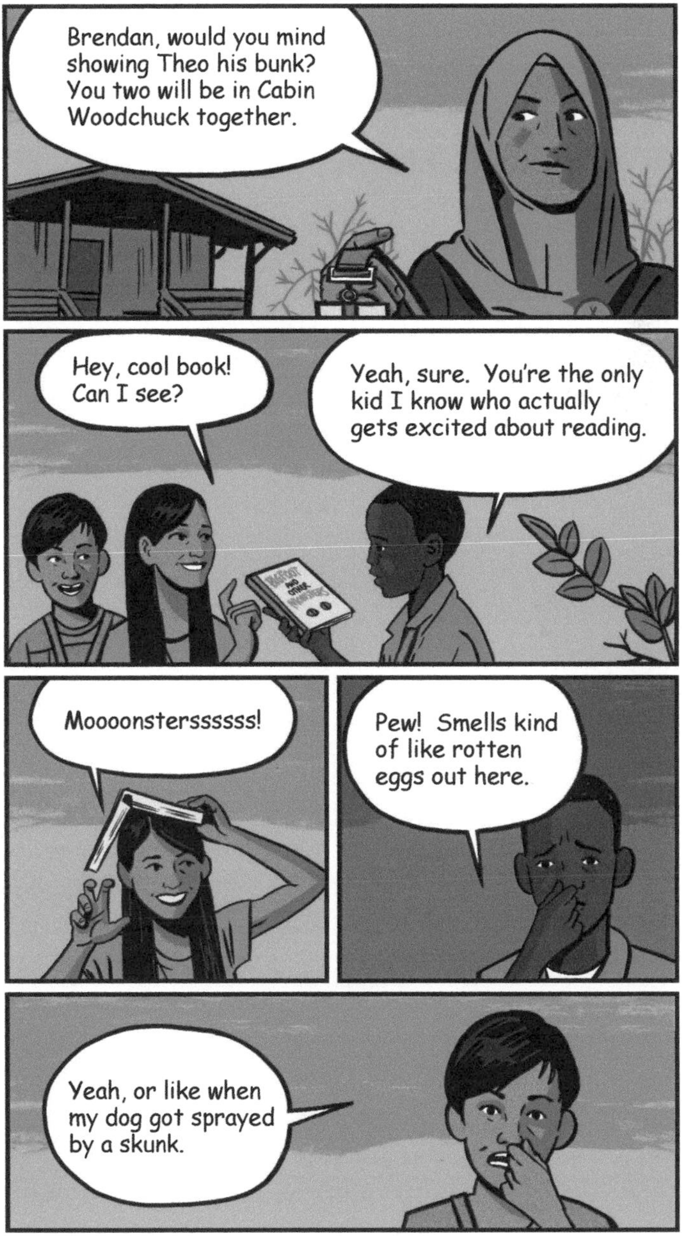
Brendan, would you mind showing Theo his bunk? You two will be in Cabin Woodchuck together.
Hey, cool book! Can I see?
Yeah, sure. You're the only kid I know who actually gets excited about reading.
Moooonstersssss!
Pew! Smells kind of like rotten eggs out here.
Yeah, or like when my dog got sprayed by a skunk.

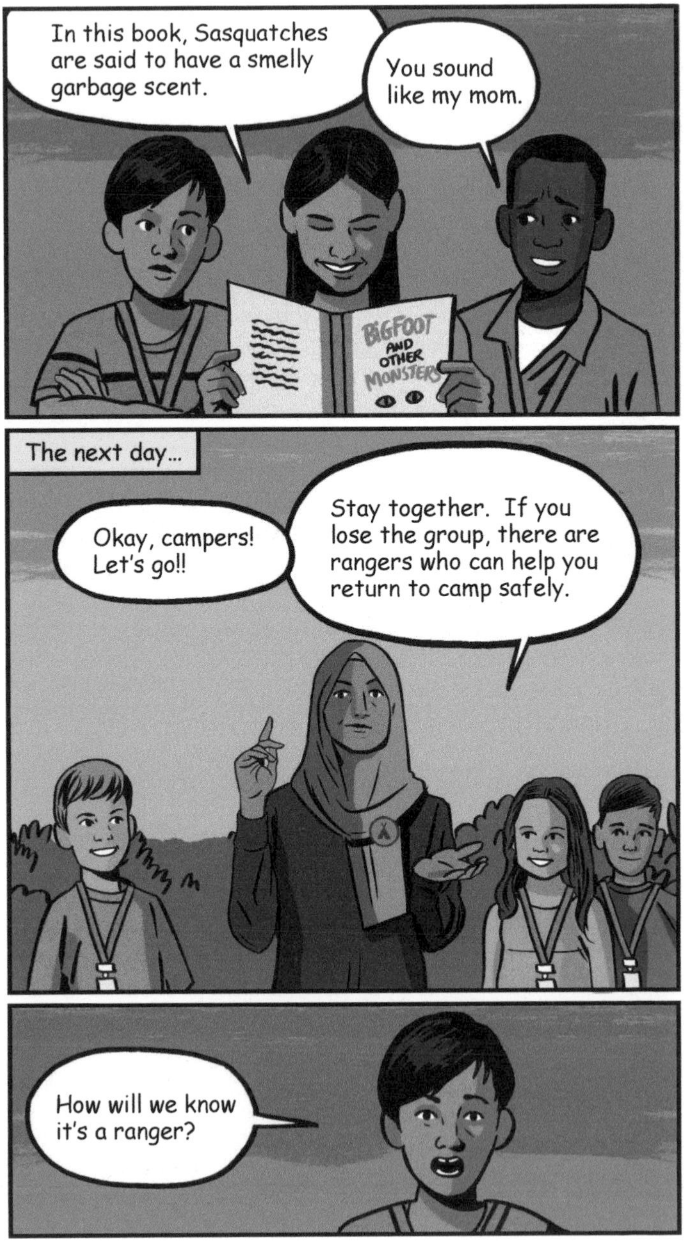
In this book, Sasquatches are said to have a smelly garbage scent.
You sound like my mom.
BIGFOOT AND OTHER MONSTERS
The next day...
Okay, campers! Let's go!!
Stay together. If you lose the group, there are rangers who can help you return to camp safely.
How will we know it's a ranger?

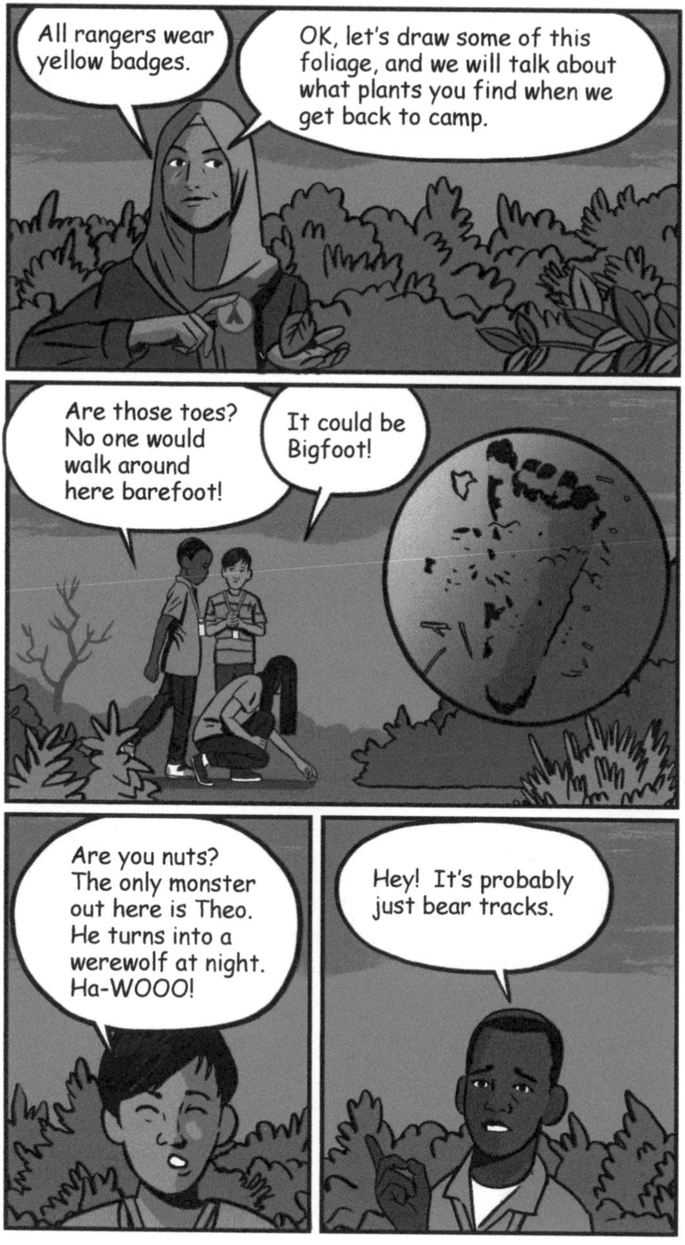
All rangers wear yellow badges.
OK, let's draw some of this foliage, and we will talk about what plants you find when we get back to camp.
Are those toes? No one would walk around here barefoot!
It could be Bigfoot!
Are you nuts? The only monster out here is Theo. He turns into a werewolf at night. Ha-WOOO!
Hey! It's probably just bear tracks.

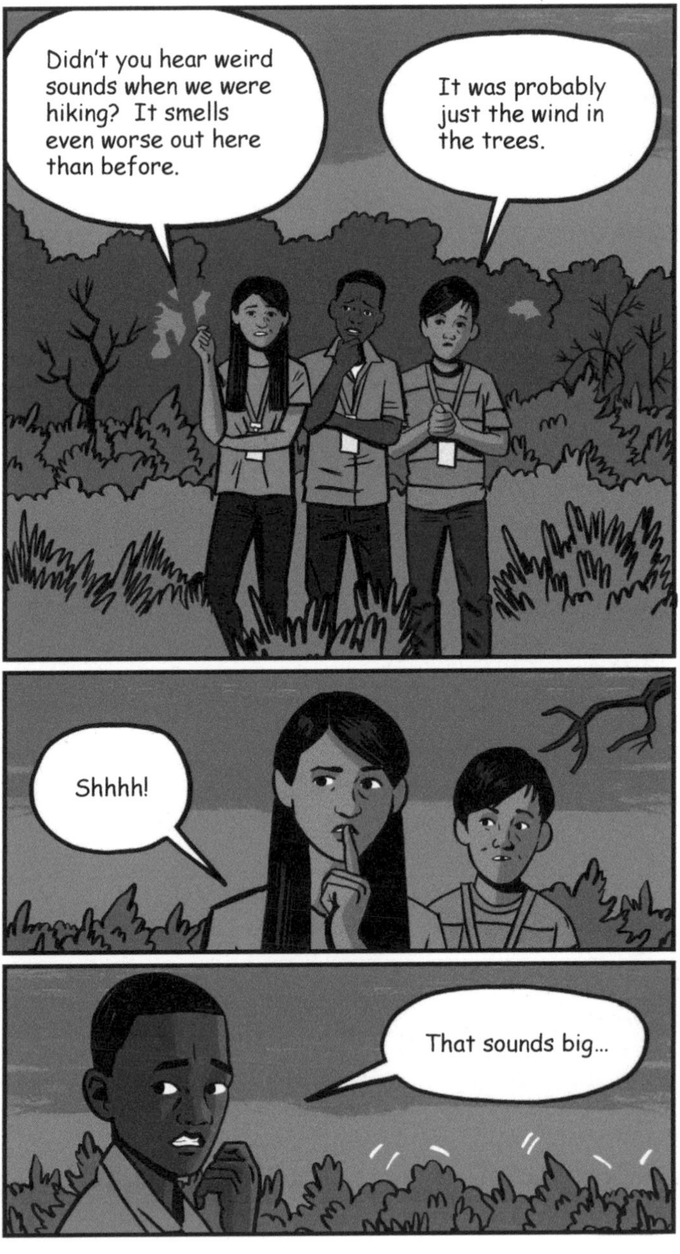
Didn't you hear weird sounds when we were hiking? It smells even worse out here than before.
It was probably just the wind in the trees.
Shhhh!
That sounds big...

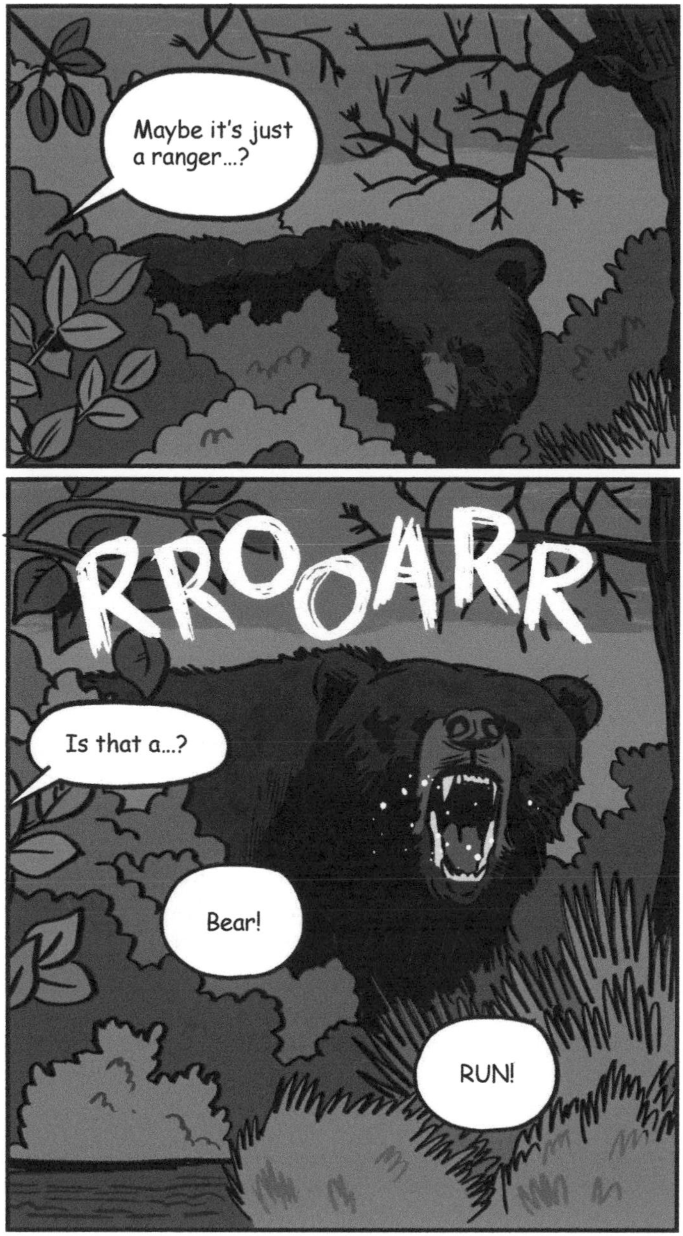
Maybe it's just a ranger...?
RROOARR
Is that a...?
Bear!
RUN!

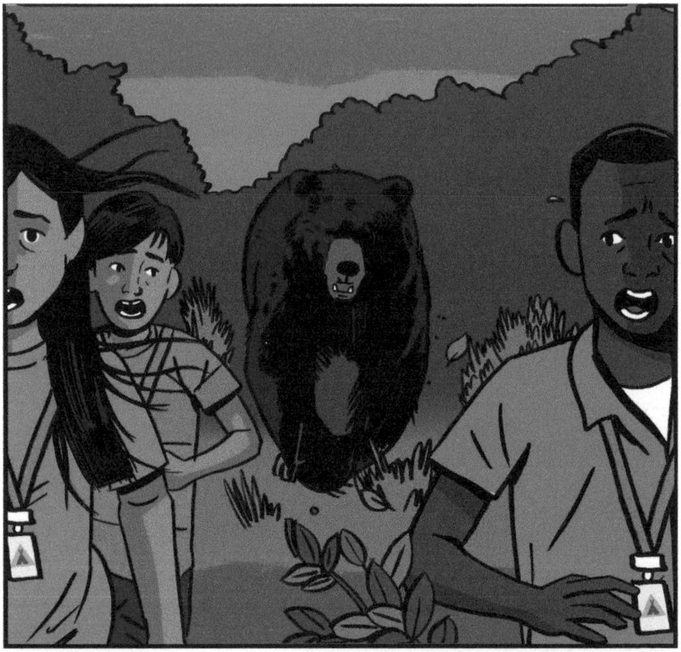

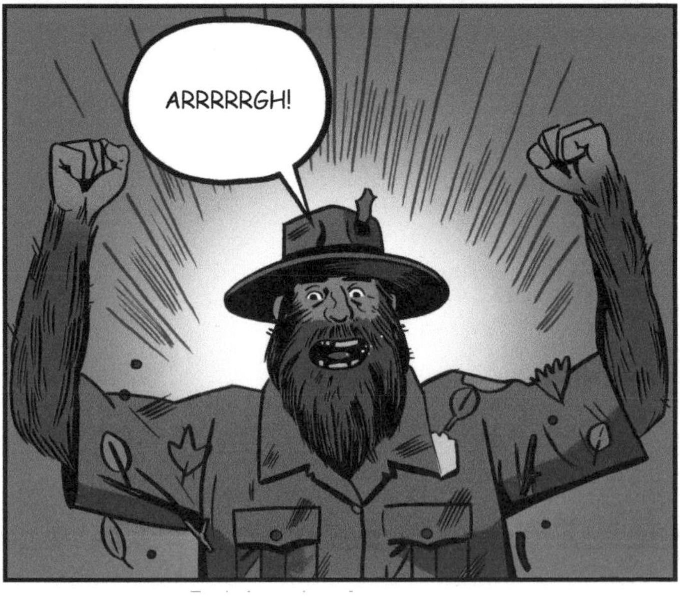
ARRRRRGH!

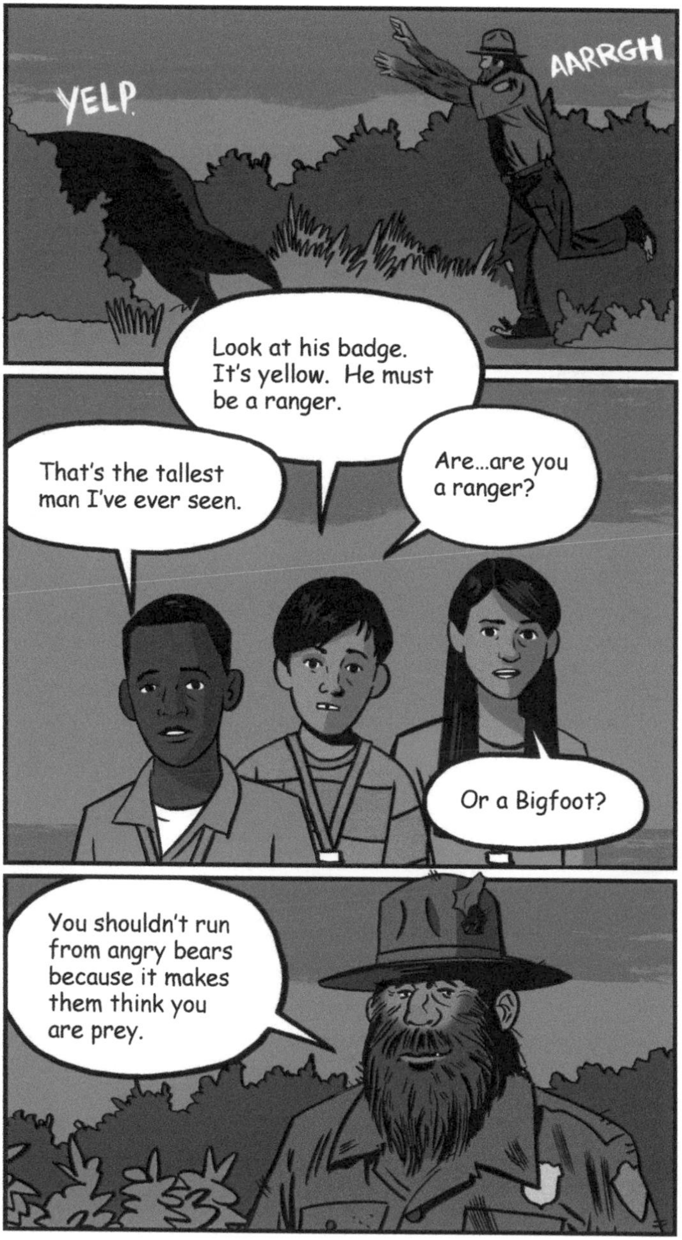
YELP
AARRGH
Look at his badge. It's yellow. He must be a ranger.
That's the tallest man I've ever seen.
Are...are you a ranger?
Or a Bigfoot?
You shouldn't run from angry bears because it makes them think you are prey.

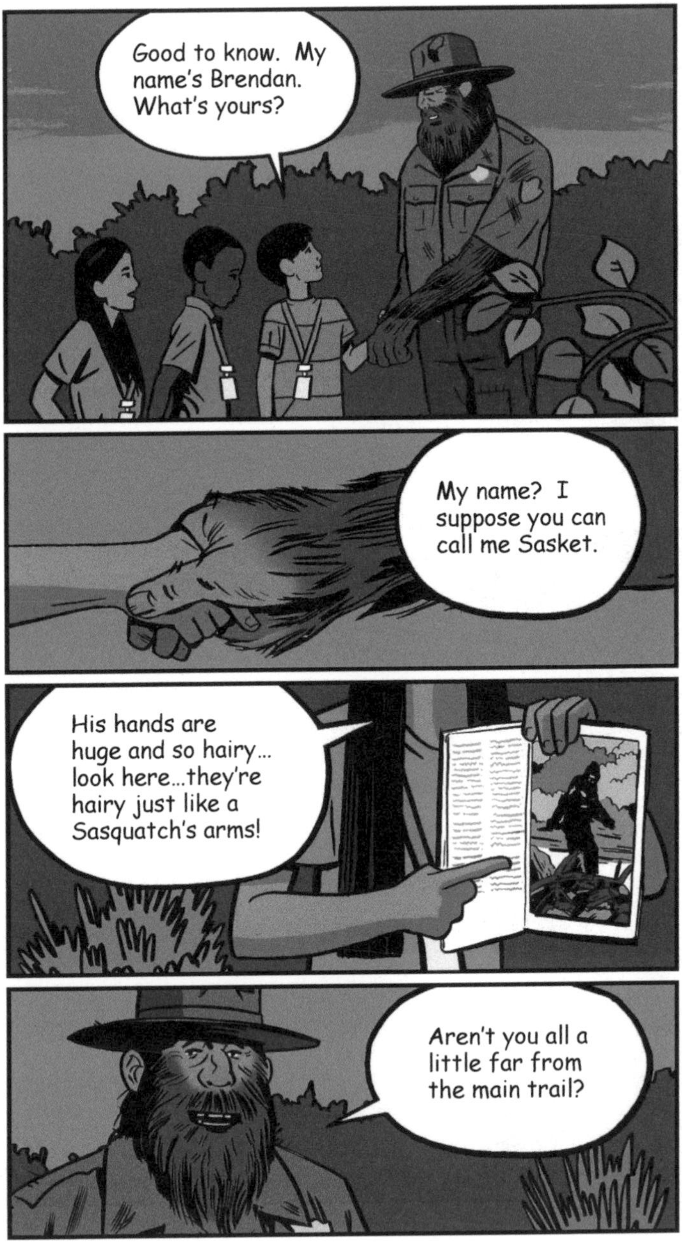
Good to know. My name's Brendan. What's yours?
My name? I suppose you can call me Sasket.
His hands are huge and so hairy... look here...they're hairy just like a Sasquatch's arms!
Aren't you all a little far from the main trail?

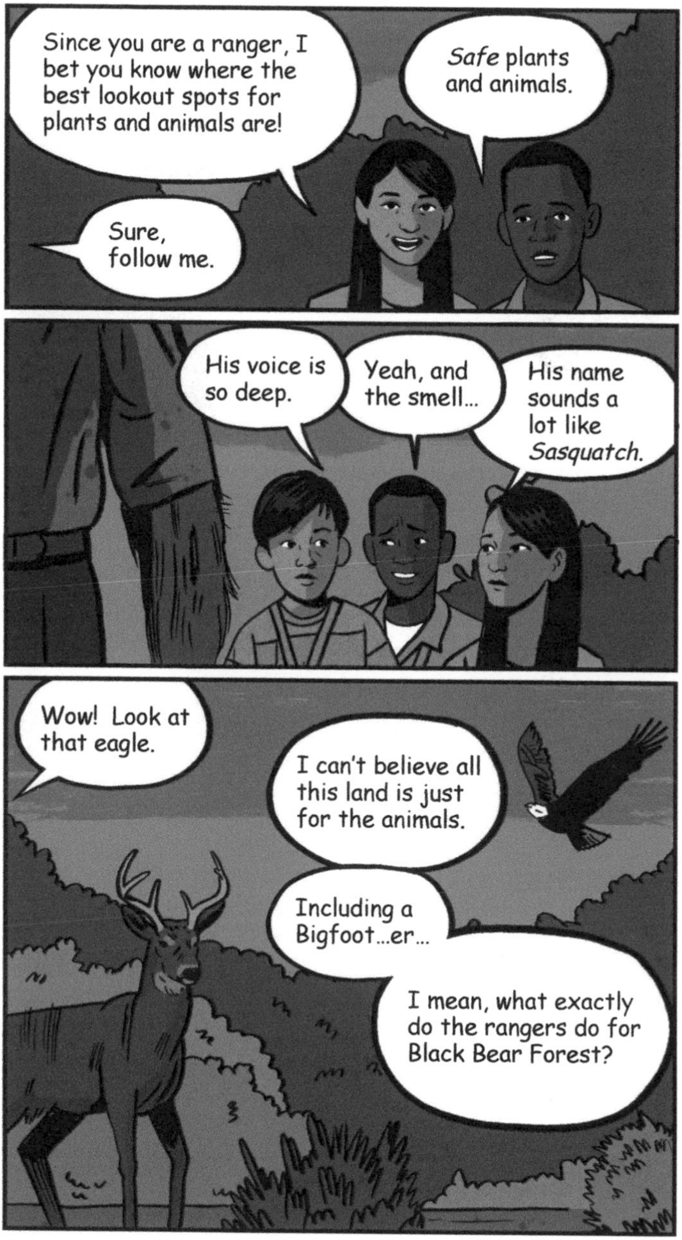
Since you are a ranger, I bet you know where the best lookout spots for plants and animals are!
Safe plants and animals.
Sure, follow me.
His voice is so deep.
Yeah, and the smell...
His name sounds a lot like *Sasquatch*.
Wow! Look at that eagle.
I can't believe all this land is just for the animals.
Including a Bigfoot...er...
I mean, what exactly do the rangers do for Black Bear Forest?

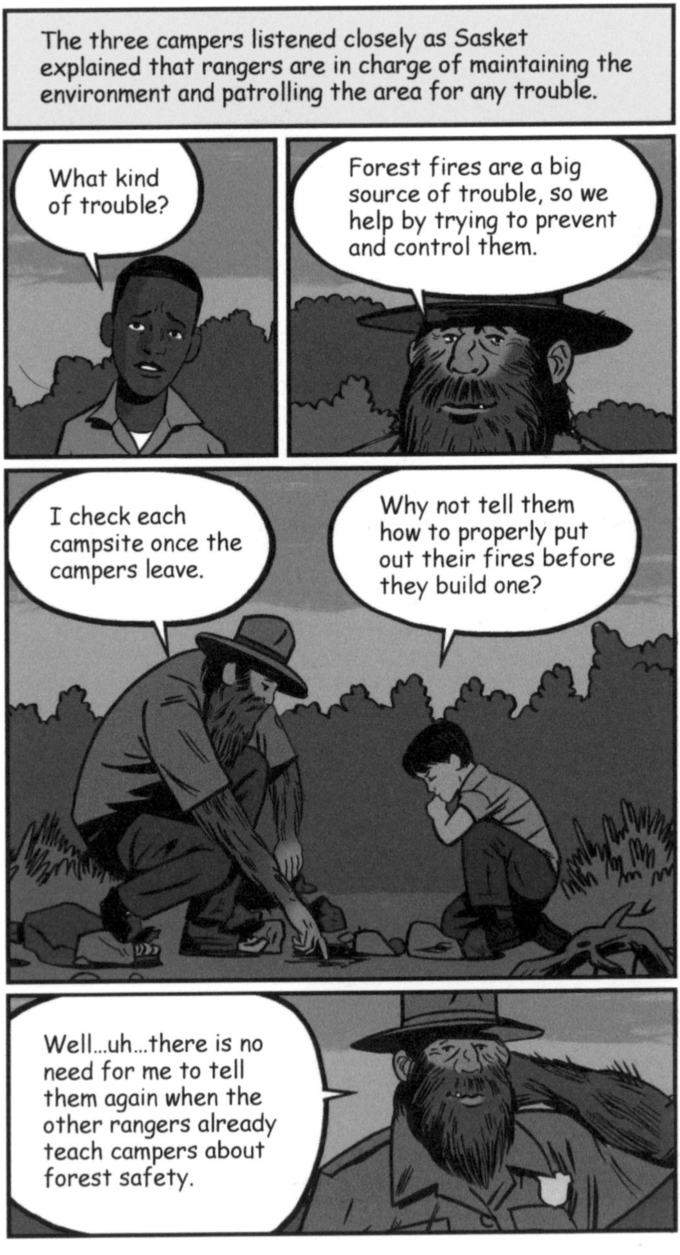
The three campers listened closely as Sasket explained that rangers are in charge of maintaining the environment and patrolling the area for any trouble.
What kind of trouble?
Forest fires are a big source of trouble, so we help by trying to prevent and control them.
I check each campsite once the campers leave.
Why not tell them how to properly put out their fires before they build one?
Well...uh...there is no need for me to tell them again when the other rangers already teach campers about forest safety.

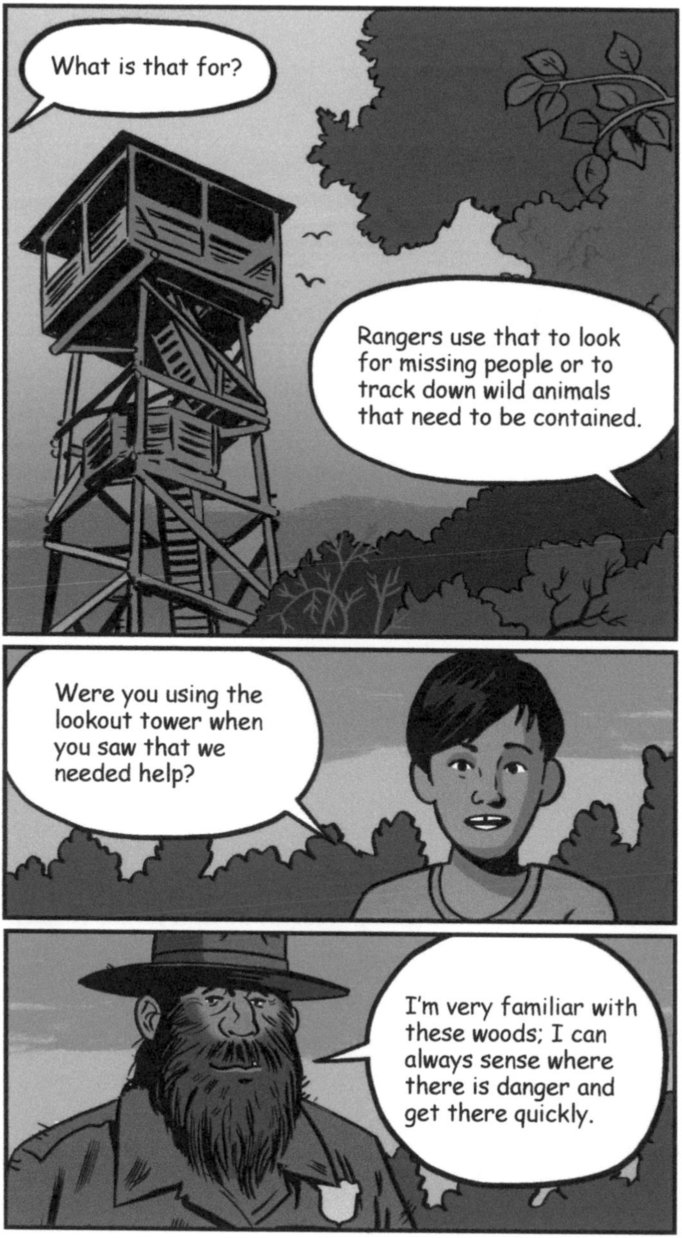
What is that for?
Rangers use that to look for missing people or to track down wild animals that need to be contained.
Were you using the lookout tower when you saw that we needed help?
I'm very familiar with these woods; I can always sense where there is danger and get there quickly.

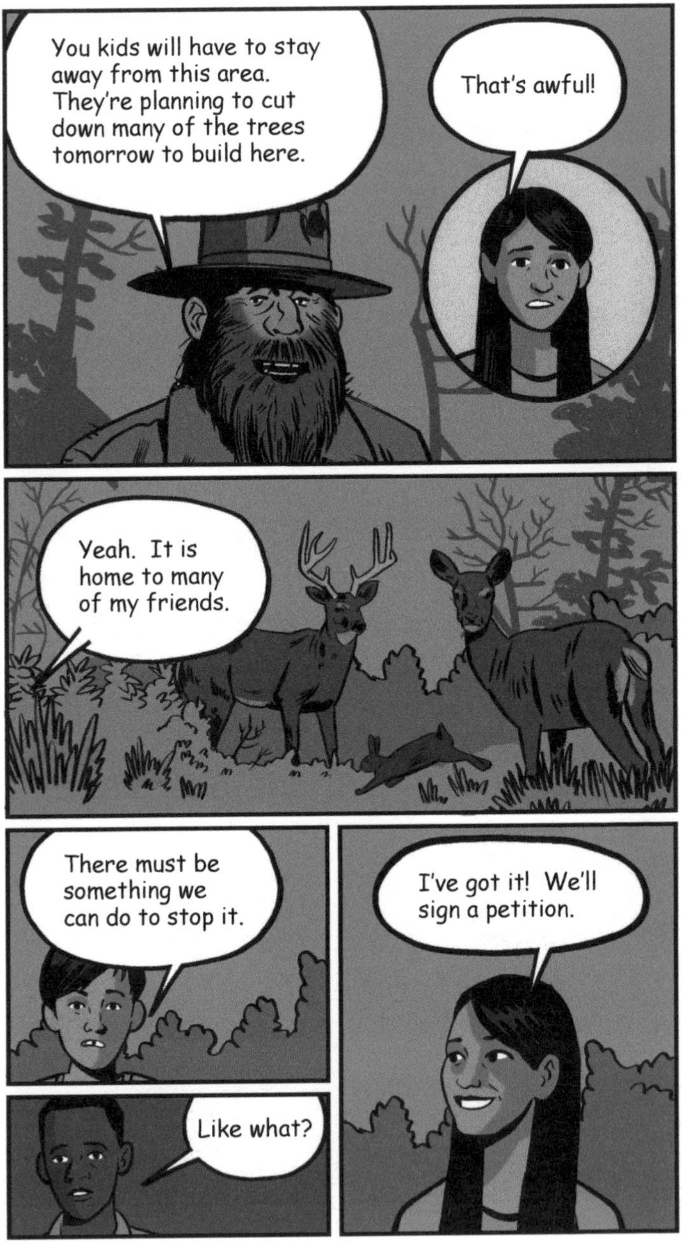
You kids will have to stay away from this area. They're planning to cut down many of the trees tomorrow to build here.
That's awful!
Yeah. It is home to many of my friends.
There must be something we can do to stop it.
Like what?
I've got it! We'll sign a petition.

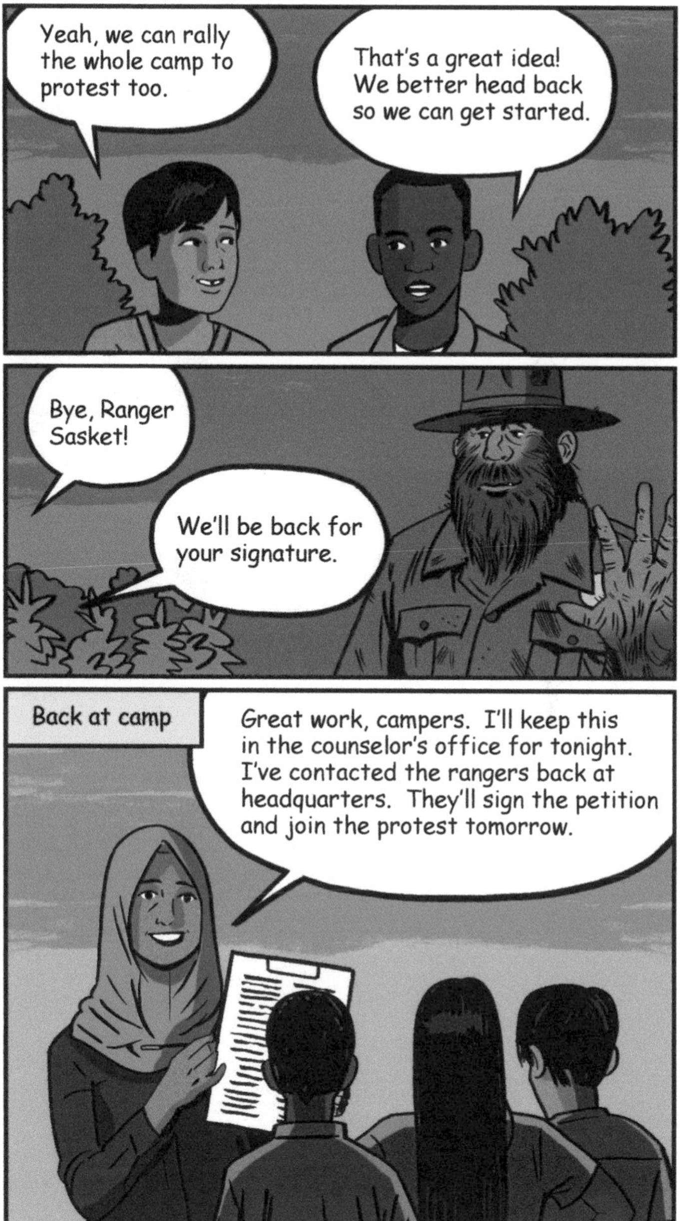
Yeah, we can rally the whole camp to protest too.
That's a great idea! We better head back so we can get started.
Bye, Ranger Sasket!
We'll be back for your signature.
Back at camp
Great work, campers. I'll keep this in the counselor's office for tonight. I've contacted the rangers back at headquarters. They'll sign the petition and join the protest tomorrow.

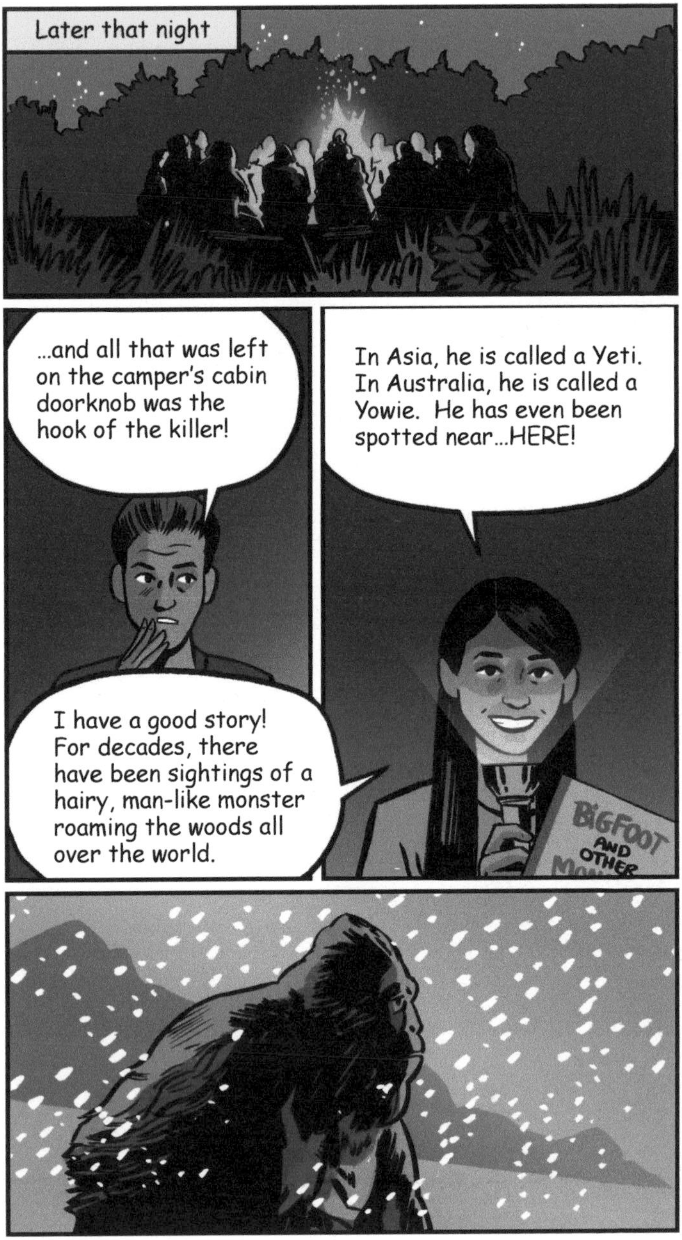
Later that night
...and all that was left on the camper's cabin doorknob was the hook of the killer!
I have a good story! For decades, there have been sightings of a hairy, man-like monster roaming the woods all over the world.
In Asia, he is called a Yeti. In Australia, he is called a Yowie. He has even been spotted near...HERE!
BIGFOOT AND OTHER

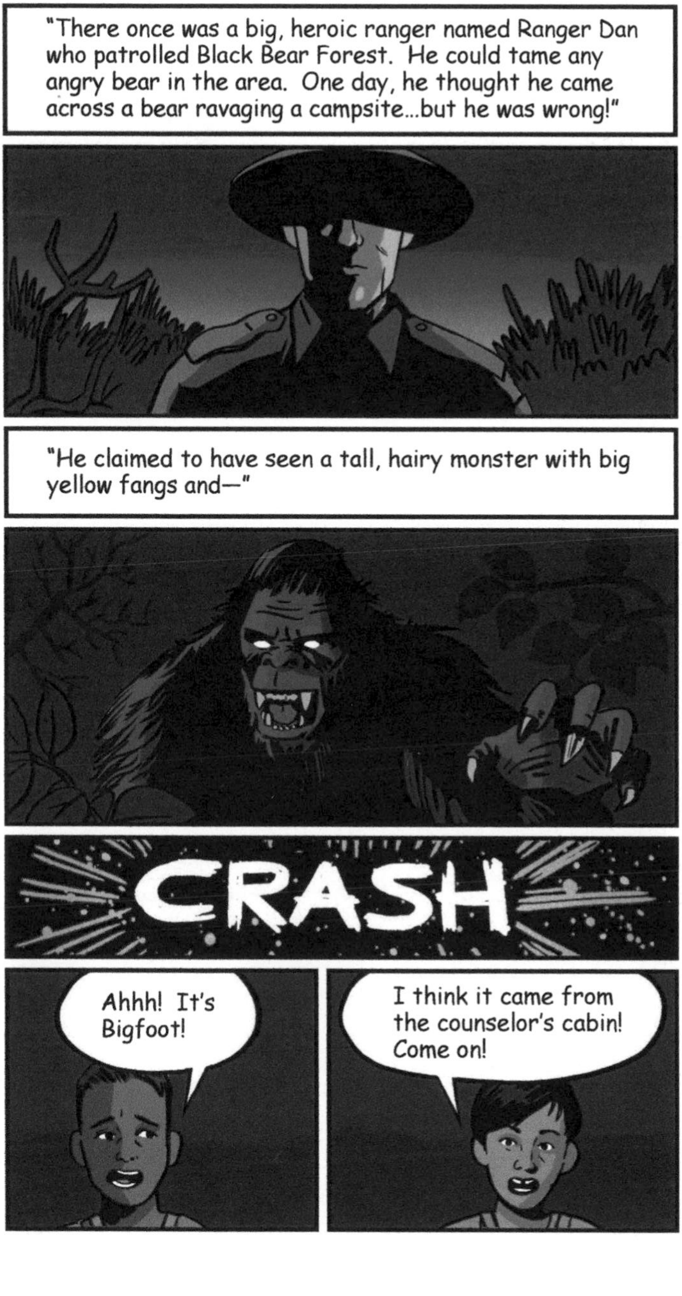
"There once was a big, heroic ranger named Ranger Dan who patrolled Black Bear Forest. He could tame any angry bear in the area. One day, he thought he came across a bear ravaging a campsite...but he was wrong!"
"He claimed to have seen a tall, hairy monster with big yellow fangs and—"
CRASH
Ahhh! It's Bigfoot!
I think it came from the counselor's cabin! Come on!

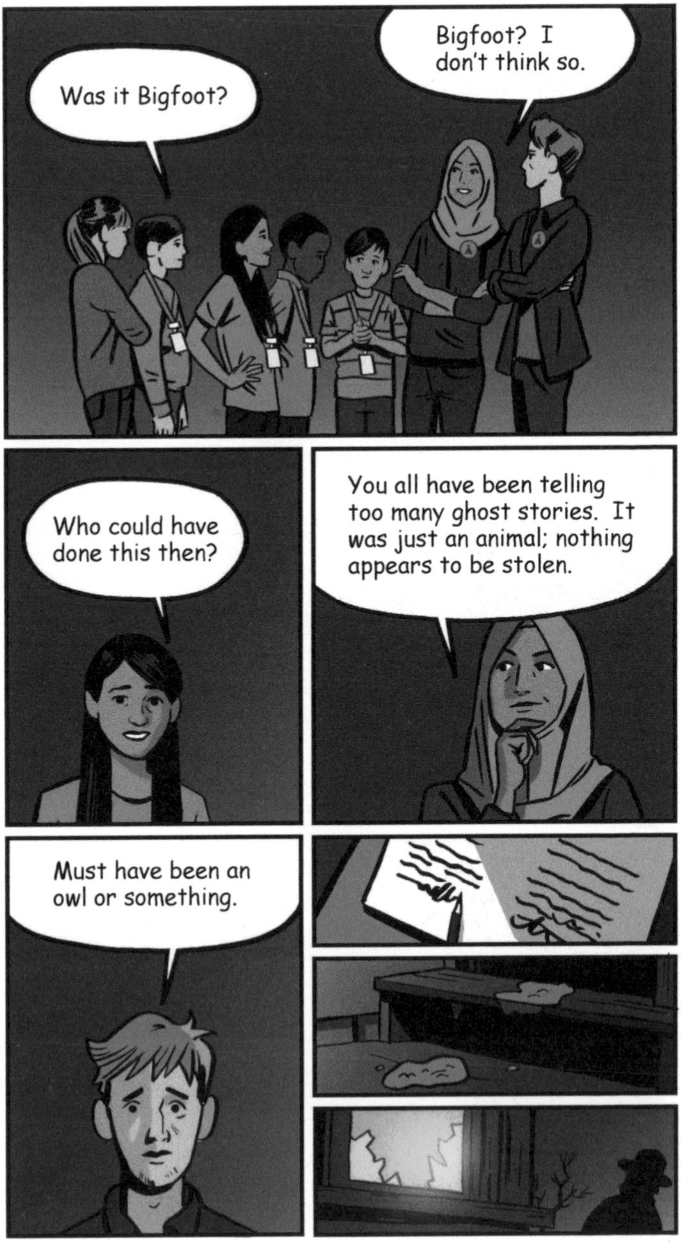
Was it Bigfoot?
Bigfoot? I don't think so.
Who could have done this then?
You all have been telling too many ghost stories. It was just an animal; nothing appears to be stolen.
Must have been an owl or something.

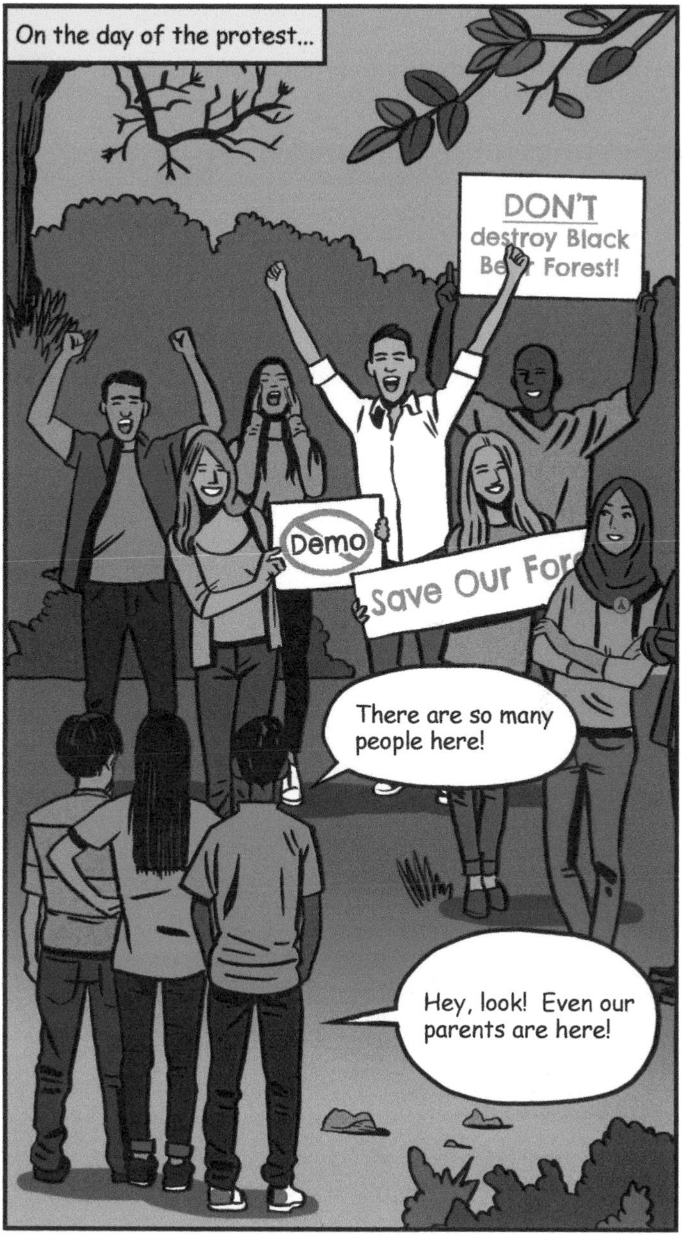
On the day of the protest...
DON'T
destroy Black
Demo
Save Our
There are so many people here!
Hey, look! Even our parents are here!

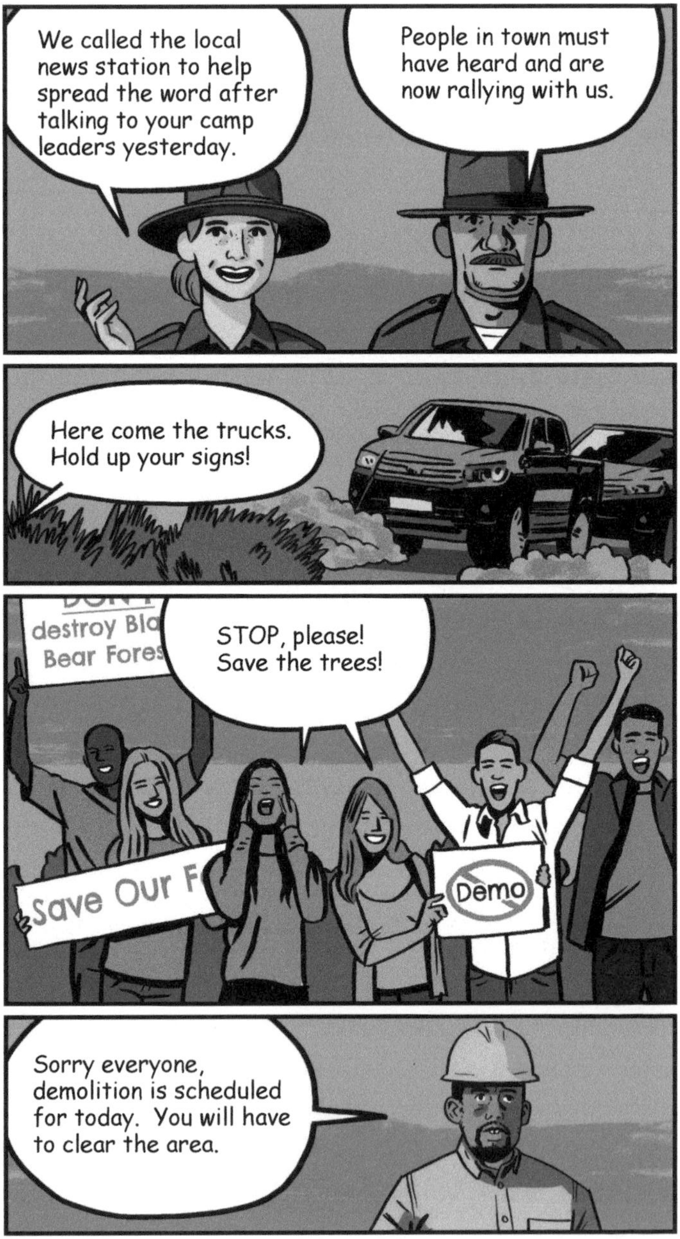
We called the local news station to help spread the word after talking to your camp leaders yesterday.
People in town must have heard and are now rallying with us.
Here come the trucks. Hold up your signs!
destroy Bla
Bear Fores
STOP, please! Save the trees!
Save Our F
Demo
Sorry everyone, demolition is scheduled for today. You will have to clear the area.

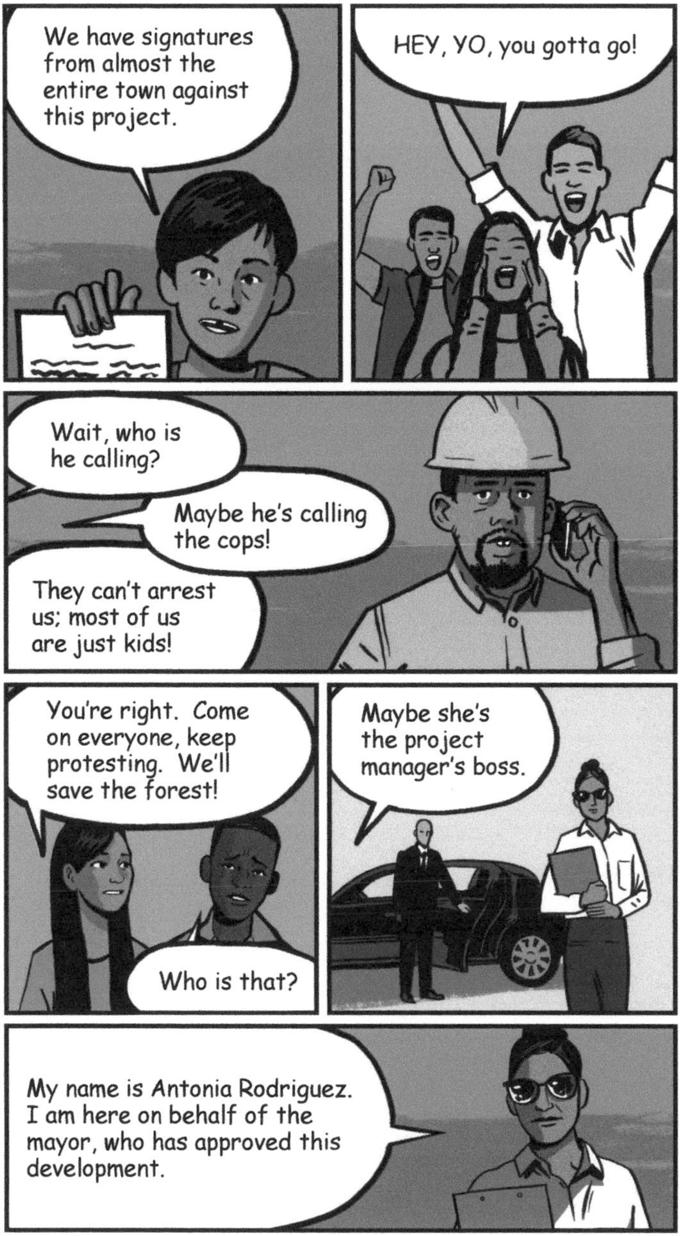
We have signatures from almost the entire town against this project.
HEY, YO, you gotta go!
Wait, who is he calling?
Maybe he's calling the cops!
They can't arrest us; most of us are just kids!
You're right. Come on everyone, keep protesting. We'll save the forest!
Who is that?
Maybe she's the project manager's boss.
My name is Antonia Rodriguez. I am here on behalf of the mayor, who has approved this development.

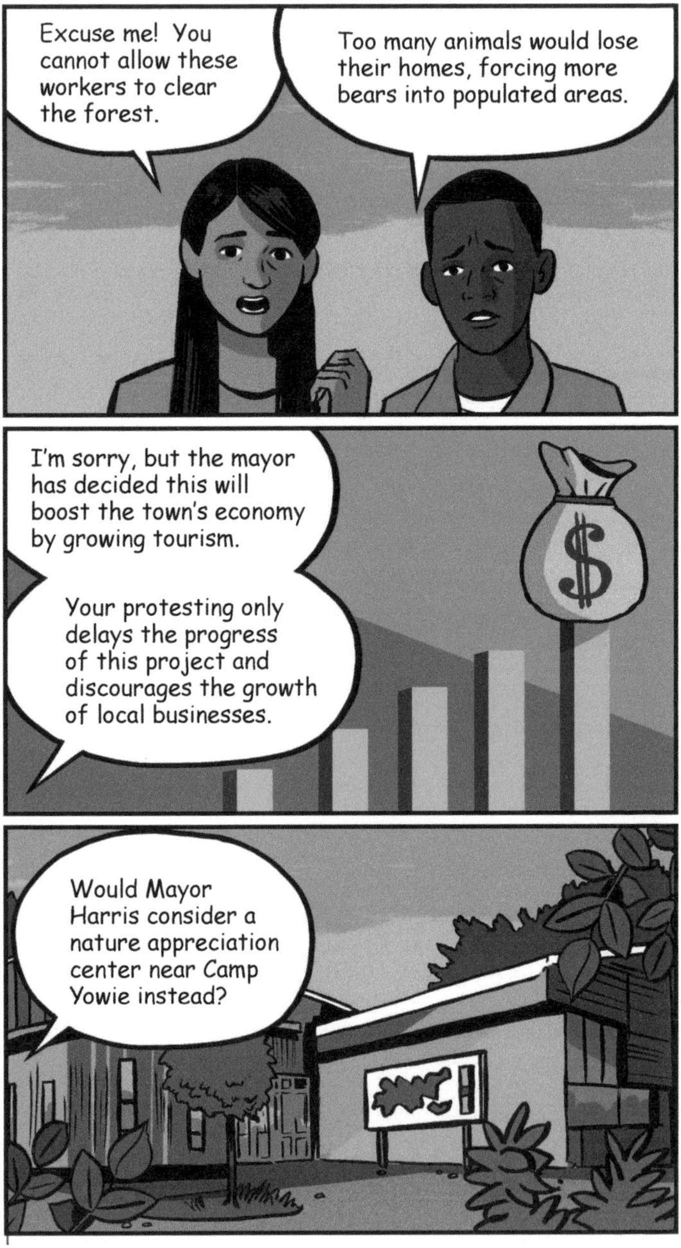
Excuse me! You cannot allow these workers to clear the forest.
Too many animals would lose their homes, forcing more bears into populated areas.
I'm sorry, but the mayor has decided this will boost the town's economy by growing tourism.
Your protesting only delays the progress of this project and discourages the growth of local businesses.
Would Mayor Harris consider a nature appreciation center near Camp Yowie instead?

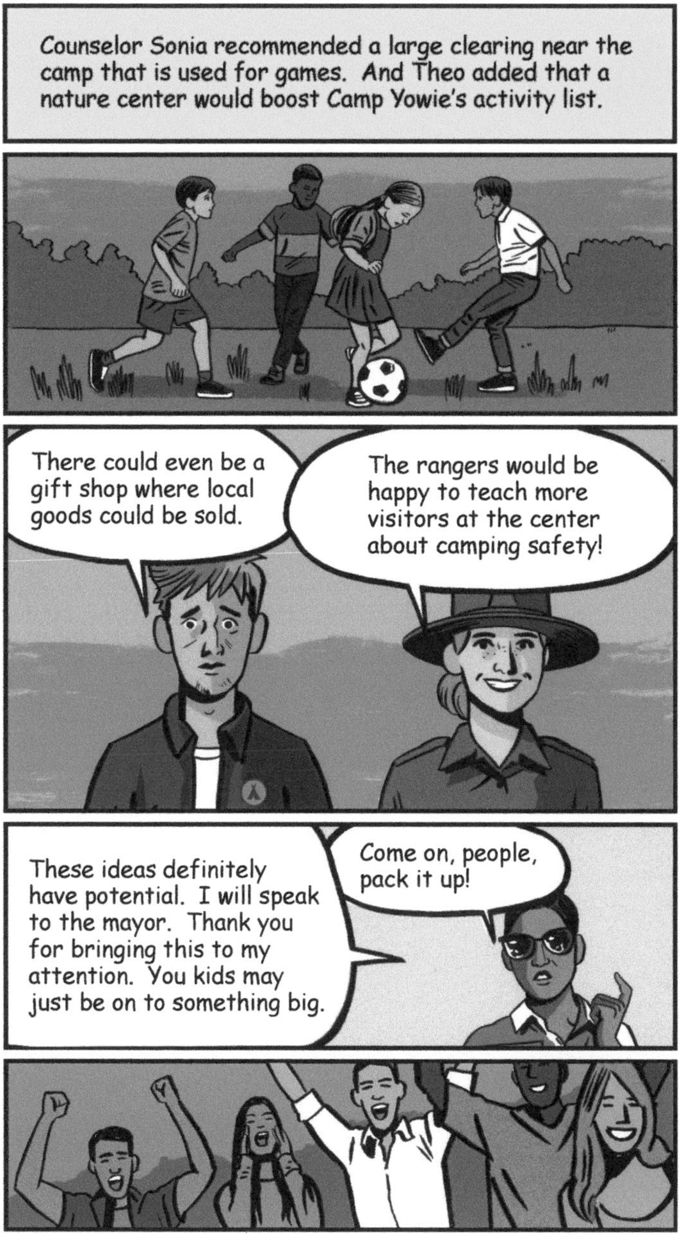
Counselor Sonia recommended a large clearing near the camp that is used for games. And Theo added that a nature center would boost Camp Yowie's activity list.
There could even be a gift shop where local goods could be sold.
The rangers would be happy to teach more visitors at the center about camping safety!
These ideas definitely have potential. I will speak to the mayor. Thank you for bringing this to my attention. You kids may just be on to something big.
Come on, people, pack it up!

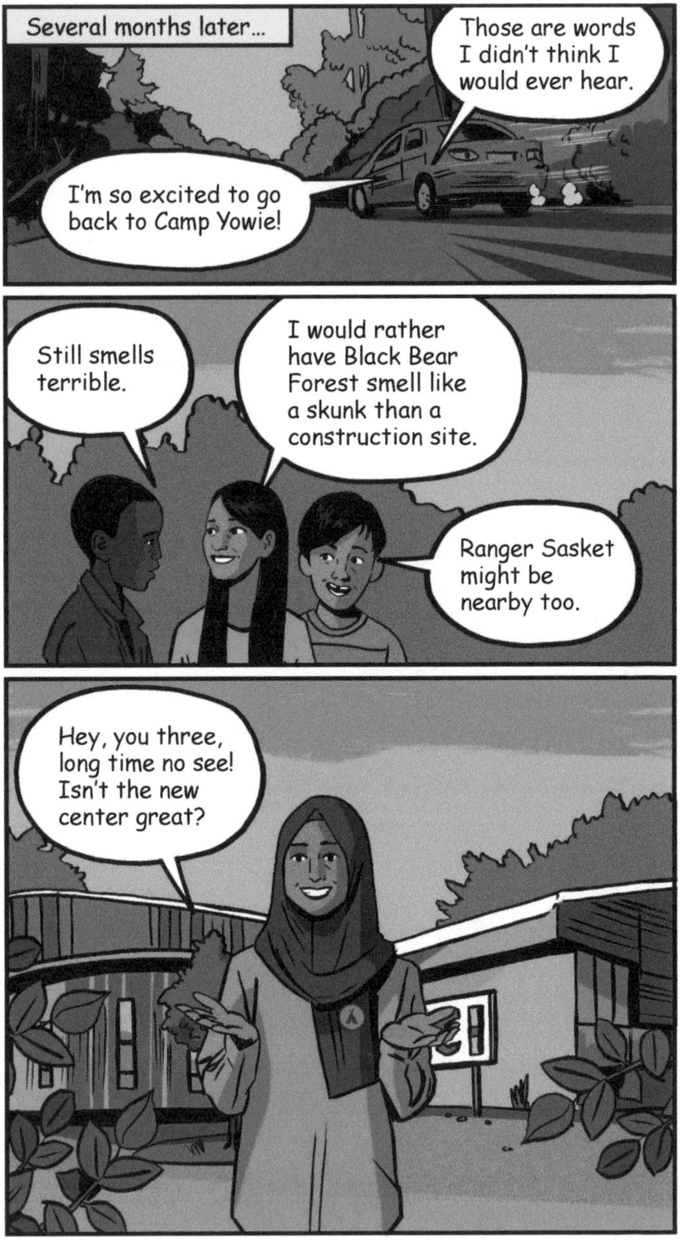

Several months later...
I'm so excited to go back to Camp Yowie!
Those are words I didn't think I would ever hear.
Still smells terrible.
I would rather have Black Bear Forest smell like a skunk than a construction site.
Ranger Sasket might be nearby too.
Hey, you three, long time no see! Isn't the new center great?

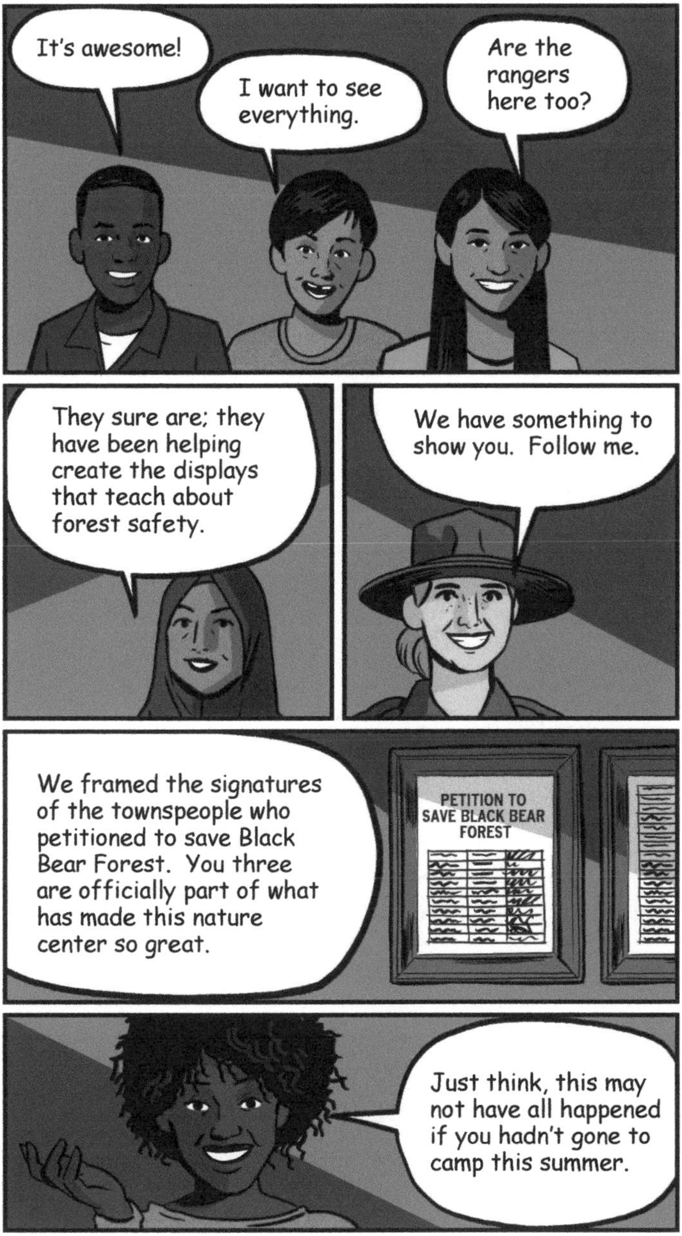
It's awesome!
I want to see everything.
Are the rangers here too?
They sure are; they have been helping create the displays that teach about forest safety.
We have something to show you. Follow me.
We framed the signatures of the townspeople who petitioned to save Black Bear Forest. You three are officially part of what has made this nature center so great.
PETITION TO SAVE BLACK BEAR FOREST
Just think, this may not have all happened if you hadn't gone to camp this summer.

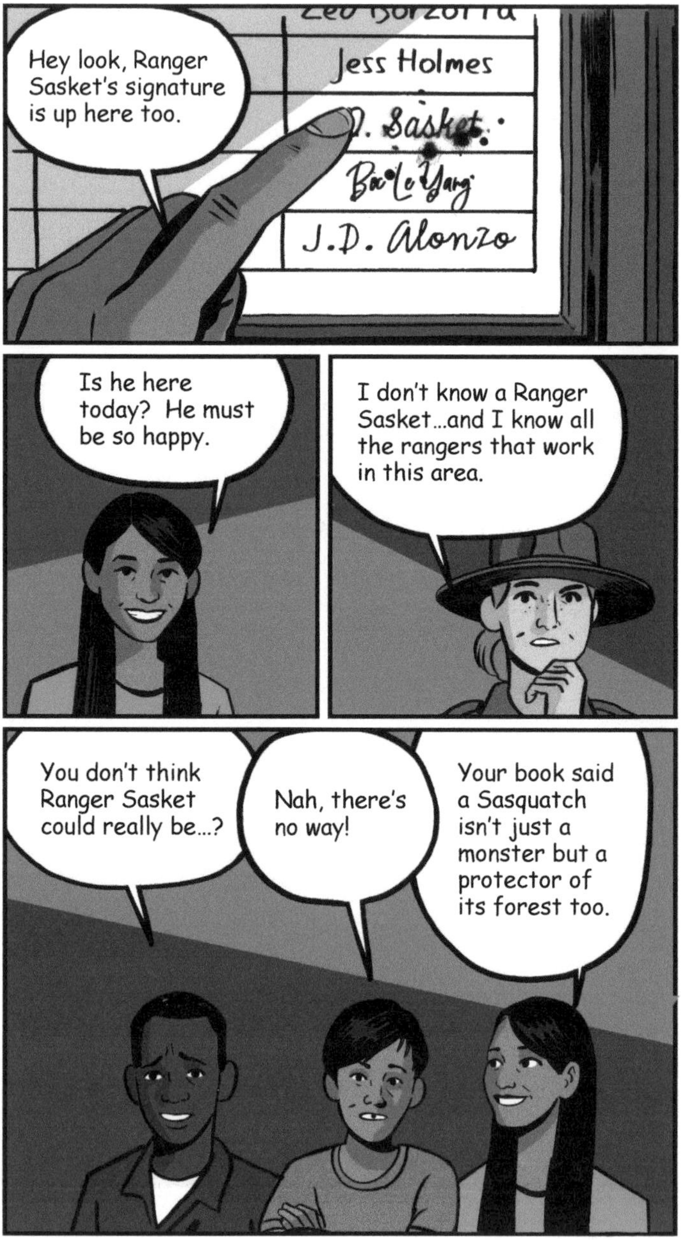
Jess Holmes
J.D. Alonzo
Hey look, Ranger Sasket's signature is up here too.
Is he here today? He must be so happy.
I don't know a Ranger Sasket...and I know all the rangers that work in this area.
You don't think Ranger Sasket could really be...?
Nah, there's no way!
Your book said a Sasquatch isn't just a monster but a protector of its forest too.

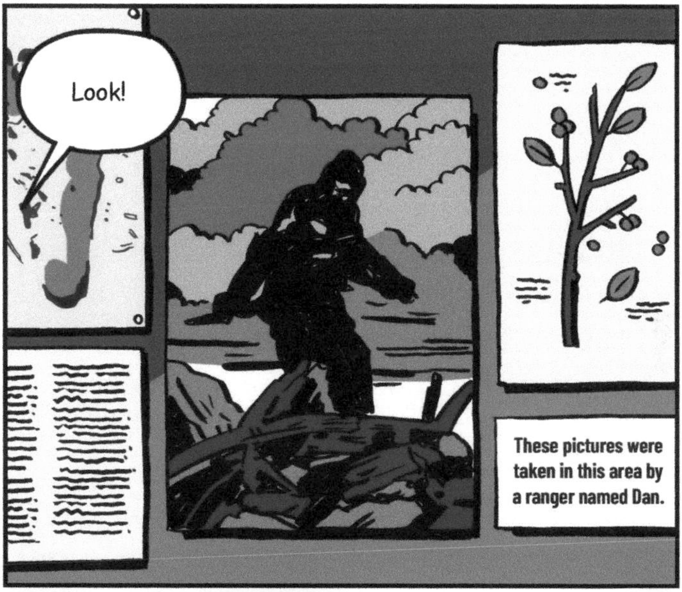
Look!
These pictures were taken in this area by a ranger named Dan.

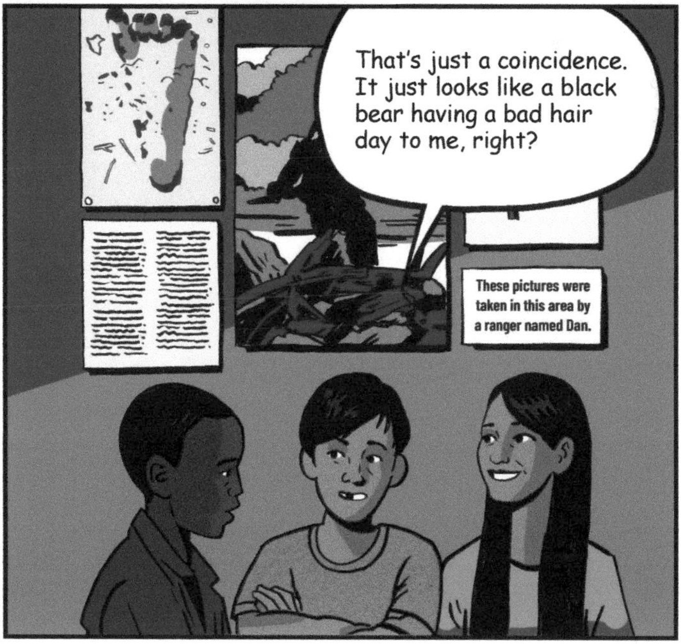
These pictures were taken in this area by a ranger named Dan.
That's just a coincidence. It just looks like a black bear having a bad hair day to me, right?

About Us

The Author

Alexandria Gold was born in Portland, Oregon, where rainy days inspired a love of creativity from a young age and stories of Bigfoot were always told around a campfire. She taught at the Academy of Art University in San Francisco. Today, she lives in Portland, where she creates art and stories for children. She still teaches for the Academy online, and she still tells stories about Bigfoot.

The Illustrator

From an early age, Chris King has taken inspiration from comic books, and some of his earliest memories are of copying pages of *Asterix the Gaul* in colored crayons. The feeling he gets from drawing with a pencil on paper is like no other. He has a degree in media production, specializing in animation and character design. Music is *always* playing when he's working.